THE HOLE TRUTH ABOUT Work

by David Lewman

POCKET BOOKS
New York   London   Toronto   Sydney   Bikini Bottom

POCKET BOOKS, a division of Simon & Schuster, Inc.
1230 Avenue of the Americas, New York, NY 10020

Copyright © 2004 by Viacom International Inc. All rights reserved.
NICKELODEON, SpongeBob SquarePants, and all related titles,
logos, and characters are trademarks of Viacom International Inc.

First published in Great Britain in 2004 by Simon & Schuster UK Ltd

All rights reserved, including the right to reproduce
this book or portions thereof in any form whatsoever.
For information address Pocket Books,
1230 Avenue of the Americas, New York, NY 10020

ISBN: 1-4165-0049-9

First Pocket Books trade paperback edition November 2004

10 9 8 7 6 5 4 3 2 1

POCKET and colophon are registered trademarks of Simon & Schuster, Inc.

Manufactured in the United States of America

For information regarding special discounts for bulk purchases, please contact
Simon & Schuster Special Sales at 1-800-456-6798 or business@simonandschuster.com

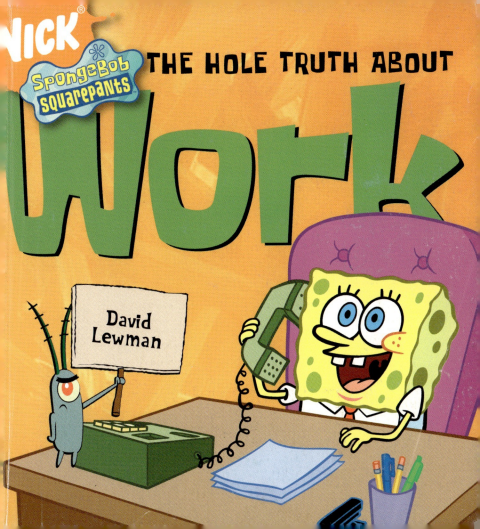

Looking to add fulfillment to your dull, dull life?

First, decide what you really want to do.

In interviews,
proudly describe
your work history.

When you're applying for a job, it's okay to show your competitive edge.

Can you reproduce by budding?
Can ya? Can ya? Huh? Can ya?

On your first day, pay close attention when your supervisor describes your duties.

You're part of my crew now, and our job is to sail around and frighten people! It'll be grueling, mind numbing and repetitive, just like daytime television.

Serve your boss well, and you'll be treated with respect and generosity.

i always come to work at 3 a.m.
This is when i count the sesame seeds.

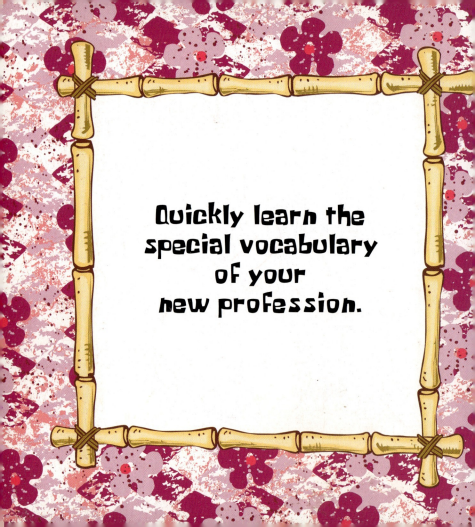

In fact, the most important rule of employment is "Think of the customer!"

i always thought
the most important rule was
"Why do today
what you can put off
until tomorrow?"

You gonna buy something or just stand there?
'Cause there's a standing fee.

Cheerfully help the customer come to a decision.

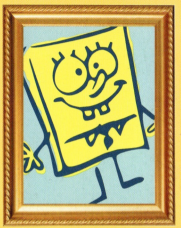

i'd like my view to be a little less yellow, if you know what i mean.

Keep abreast of
your company's latest
special offers.

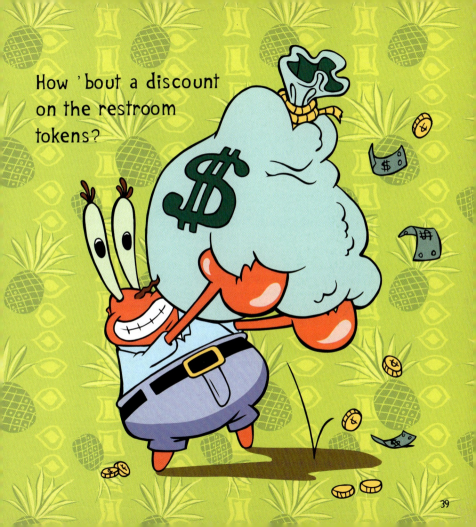

Speak

Management is eager to hear your fresh, new ideas!

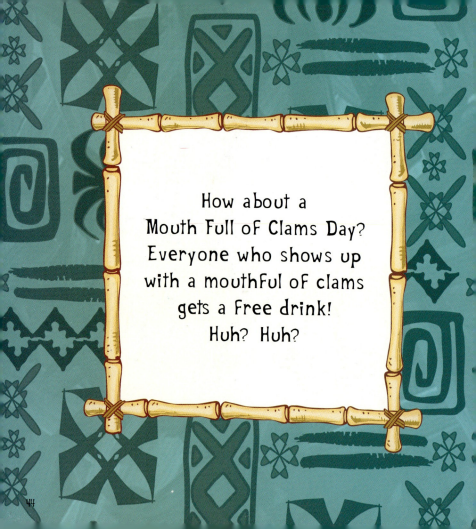

No one's taken a break at the Krusty Krab since the chum famine of '59!

Give your employer plenty of notice before taking a day off.

Personally, i like to spend my day off at the best place in the universe — the Krusty Krab!

How am I supposed to enjoy your day off if you come to work anyway?!

To constantly improve, the great employee counts on performance reviews from his boss.

But i've never reviewed anything.
Except for the foreign exercise videos
my cousin sent me.

A customer ordered a medium soda and i gave him a large! i gave him a large! i've soiled the good Krusty Krab name! Soiled it! Soiled it! Soiled it!

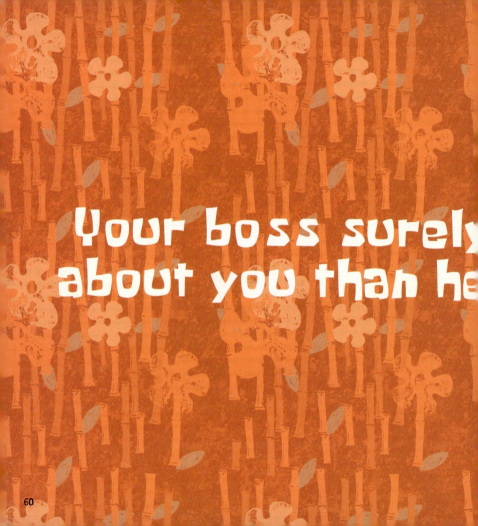

cares much more
does about money.

You really havent got any
brains at all, have you, son?

Have you ever noticed
salt shakers?
i mean, ya Fill 'em up
every night at closing
and, i mean, where does
it all go? Huh?

if you have to choose between being loyal to your company and stretching the truth, be loyal.

Hooray for lying!

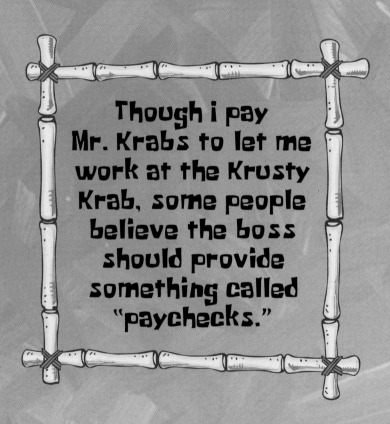

He owes us for all the precious irretrievable moments we've wasted in this trash heap!

i got a bad feelin'
in the pit of me wallet.

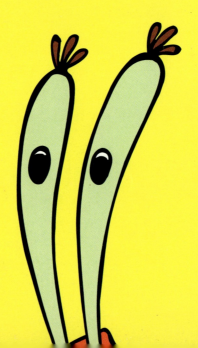

Some people even think your boss should pay something called "benefits."

When your coworkers collect for charity, always give generously.

In case you've forgotten, here's how things work. I order the food, you cook the food, then the customer gets the food. We do that for 40 years and then we die! Sounds like a pretty good deal to me, whadaya say, pal?

Boy, those Krabby Patty fumes must have got to your head. Borrow Squidward's gas mask, then get right back to work.

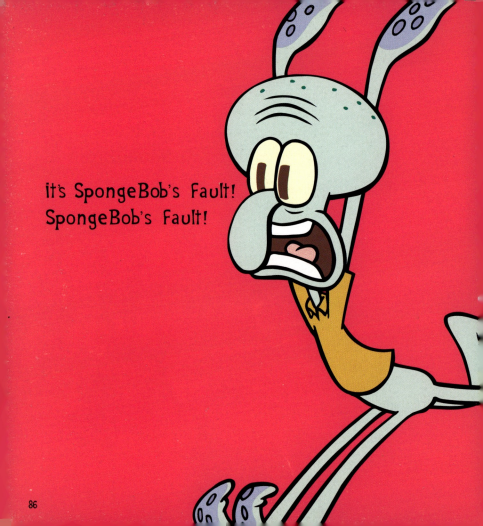

All you really have to do is work hard every day.

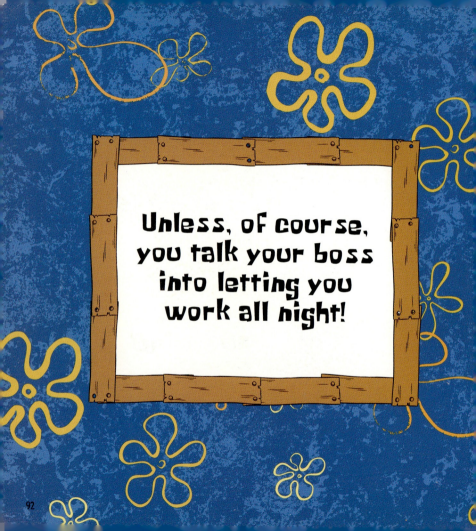

it'll be just like a sleepover only we'll be sweaty and covered with grease!

Remember, your job is what you make it!